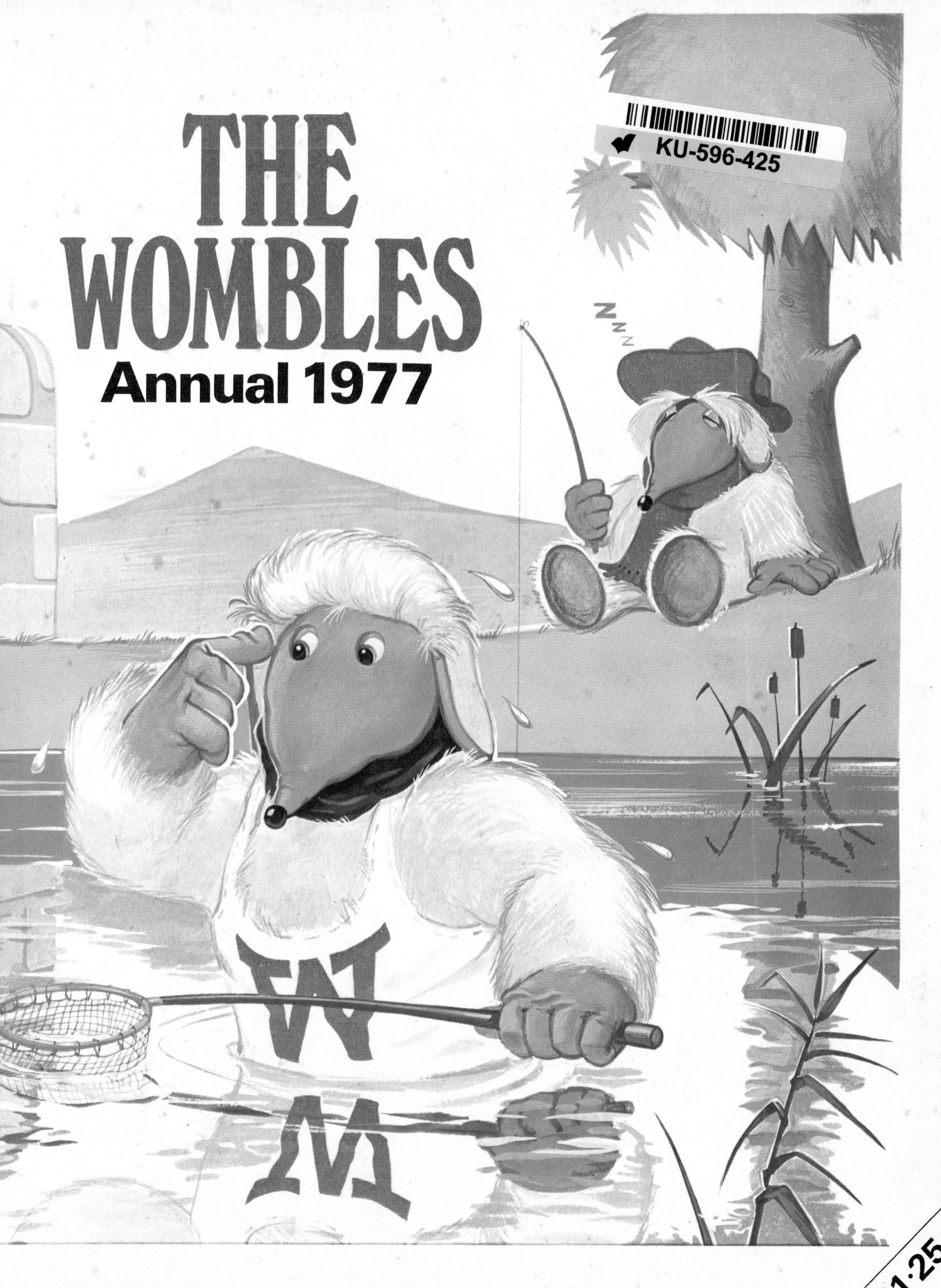
THE WOMBLES
Annual 1977
KU-596-425
£1·25

Contents

STORIES

FEATURES

Drawn from Ivor Woods' original film puppets by David Fryer

Published in Great Britain by
World Distributors (Manchester) Limited,
P.O. Box 111, 12 Lever Street,
Manchester. M60 1TS.
Printed in Great Britain by
Jarrold & Sons Ltd., Norwich.
SBN 7235 0365 6

Tobermory, Cousin Yellowstone and the Bleepers and Bloopers.

"Dear me," said Great Uncle Bulgaria, "a letter from Cousin Yellowstone Womble in America. And a very LONG letter too."

"Probably got nothing else to do but write letters, and very expensive they are to send as well," said Tobermory.

"Cousin Yellowstone runs a very efficient burrow," said Great Uncle Bulgaria, his old eyes twinkling a little, as he knew that Tobermory was rather jealous of the American Womble. "However, now I come to read it, I see that it's a story, more than a letter. Tobermory, be a good Womble and ask Madame Cholet if she will make some of her special grass and bramble buns for tonight and perhaps some daisy cream shakes and we'll have a little feast when tidying-up work is over and I will read this story to everybody."

"Oh, very well. Lot of fuss about a letter!" mumbled Tobermory. And off he went.

So that evening everybody gathered together in the Playroom, while Great Uncle Bulgaria settled himself in his rocking chair and began to read aloud.

"Dear Great Uncle Bulgaria and all my Wimbledon Womble relations.

"We have been having an exciting time here. As you know, Yellowstone Park is very, very big indeed, so my Wombles are always busy clearing up after those untidy Human Beings. Well, last week young Idaho Womble brought back to the burrow something the like of which we had never seen before. It was a simply enormous sheet of very thin plastic with strange markings on it, and it had all kinds of tiny bits of electric parts and pieces attached to it. We didn't know what to make of it at all.

"Young Idaho managed to get it into our storeroom, where it took up a great deal of space. We decided to examine this 'thing' the next day.

"However, in the middle of the night something most unusual happened. The 'thing' BEGAN TO MAKE NOISES. I was fast asleep when suddenly I heard *'bleep-bleep-bleep-bloop'.* I don't mind admitting that my fur stood up on end. So very, very carefully I went to take a look. Our storeroom was full of little flashing lights!

" 'What is it, Cousin Yellowstone?' whispered a scared little voice behind me, and there was young Idaho with his fur all up in prickles and his eyes as round as buttons.

" 'Nothing to worry about,' I said sternly. 'I was – er – just checking that – er – the thing was not too damaged. And as you can see it is in splendid working order. Return to your bunk immediately, young Womble. You have a busy day ahead of you.'

" 'Yes Cousin Yellowstone,' replied Idaho, looking mightily relieved. 'But I do wish we weren't *quite* so busy. The Park is so very large that it's not easy to keep it clear and clean. And the wind is starting to blow, which means that we'll have more to do than ever . . . '

" 'Which is why you need all the rest you can get. Off with you, young Womble.'

"Away he scampered, leaving me with this strange, softly-bleeping-making-lights 'thing'. Well, a Womble who is in charge of a burrow has to be able to look after all that may befall, so for the rest of the night I was very busy in the store-room and in our library. And by sun-up I thought I knew quite a lot about this weird and wonderful object. But how could my Wombles make good use of it? It was a difficult and worrying problem. So I had a long, long sleep.

"While a Womble sleeps, his brain is often very busy, and when I woke up I knew what I had to do. I sent for a squad of young working Wombles and gave them instructions, and for the next twenty-four hours or so they were going every which-way. Which means their

paws hardly touched the ground. The sun-up after that we were ready. All the bleepers and bloopers had been removed from the 'thing' and the 'thing' itself had been carried out of the burrow and into the open. Attached to it were several very long lengths of cord, which in turn were tied most firmly to a shopping trolley. The kind that Human Beings use in their supermarkets. In the trolley was Idaho. His fur was a bit prickly, but he was doing his best to be brave.

"I made a little speech saying how courageous he was and what I wanted him to do. Then I gave a signal and my special squad of Wombles started to use all the air-pumps we had brought from our storehouse. Slowly but steadily the thin grey plastic thing started to ripple up and down and then to swell. It grew larger and larger and LARGER. All my Wombles went *'OOOOOOOH'* for the 'thing' was turning into a gigantic grey balloon.

" 'Hold very tight,' I ordered the young Wombles who were holding on to the cords, 'and when I say ease out, EASE OUT.'

"I gave the order and slowly young Idaho rose into the air. Up and up he went into the early morning sky.

"It was a great moment in our Yellowstone Burrow History! I raised my right paw. They all held on tightly to their cords and young Idaho, who was now way up over the Park, got out the telescope which Great Uncle Bulgaria had given to me years back and put it to his eyes.

"He turned around, a smallish figure against the sky, and then pointed. He was showing us where the high wind had left the most trash which needed to be tidied-up. We had, at long last, got our own Womble Trash Detector. It was a great, GREAT moment!"

Great Uncle Bulgaria paused at this point and looked at all his Wimbledon Wombles, who not only had eyes as round as buttons, but who had also quite forgotten to take a bite of their buns or a sip of their daisy shakes for some minutes.

"However," continued Great Uncle Bulgaria, returning to the letter, "not all the problems have been solved. What do we do with the bleeper-bloopers, and besides being a balloon what is this 'thing' we American Wombles have tidied-up? We feel there is probably only one Womble in the entire world who can answer this and we look forward to his speedy reply. Over to you Tobermory.

"This is Cousin Yellowstone signing off."

Everybody, including Great Uncle Bulgaria, turned to look at Tobermory. Tobermory, who for some

time had been making notes on the back of an envelope, spoke up.

"It's quite simple really," he said. "What these American Wombles have tidied-up is a weather balloon. Human Beings send 'em up with all these bleepers and bloopers on 'em and the bleepers and bloopers send back signals to the ground about tornadoes and storms and all the rest of it. HOWEVER, it does seem to me that as these bleeper things aren't doing anything much, except sitting in this store place, that they could be put to a much better use."

"Such as?" enquired Great Uncle Bulgaria.

"Well," said Tobermory cautiously, "I'm not promising, mind, but if Cousin Yellowstone sends some of these bleepers to me I might be able to work out a way for us Wombles in Wimbledon to signal direct to our American cousins in Yellowstone Park. And what's more," Tobermory added, "it'd be a lot cheaper and easier than writing those long letters!"

"Tobermory," said Great Uncle Bulgaria, getting out of his rocking chair, "you are a great credit to us Wimbledon Wombles. And, I may say, there is a PS to Cousin Yellowstone's letter. He says, 'We just wish we had Tobermory here in the USA to help us solve all our problems. But, Bulgaria, I don't believe you'd ever let him go, would you?' Well, would we?"

"*No. Never,*" everybody shouted.

And for once in his life Tobermory actually smiled! Then he hurried off to his Workshop to do more sums about how to make the best use of 'the - thing - and - its - bleepers - and -bloopers'.

Which Busy Womble?

One of the young Wombles has had a really busy day, as you can see with all the things collected on Wimbledon Common. If you rearrange the initial letters of all the objects, you will discover the Womble's name.

Answers on page 76

GREAT UNCLE BULGARIA'S BIRTHDAY

One morning as Great Uncle Bulgaria woke up he suddenly had the feeling that today was rather special. He tried hard to think why . . . and then suddenly there was a knock on the door and in trooped Bungo, Wellington and Orinoco.

"Happy birthday!" they chorused, and each put a present on Great Uncle Bulgaria's bed.

"I managed to find a copy of today's *Times!*" cried Bungo proudly. "A gentleman forgot it as he ran to catch his train!"

"I haven't had a new paper for ages!" beamed Great Uncle Bulgaria. "Thank you, my dear Bungo!"

"I have helped Tobermory to mend your Atlas of the World!" said Orinoco. "It was getting quite torn with its constant use with every young Womble choosing a name from it. Do you like the new cover?"

"I do indeed," smiled the oldest Womble. "You have made a very neat job, Orinoco. It will last for a great deal longer now."

"I picked you a basket of mushrooms for your breakfast," said Wellington shyly. "There are still a few left, but Madame Cholet is doing the rest for your breakfast."

"How kind!" murmured Great Uncle Bulgaria, looking very pleased.

Just then there was a knock on the door and in walked Madame Cholet and Alderney carrying a breakfast tray.

"Happy birthday," they both cried, as Alderney set the tray on the bed.

"You deserve breakfast in bed on your birthday," smiled Madame Cholet, "and as an extra present, I have mended the holes in your shawl and re-covered your footstool with a lovely piece of velvet that Wellington found. Now eat up your breakfast, it's your favourite!"

And indeed it was, there was toadstool scramble with mushrooms on fried moss bread, dandelion toast and bracken marmalade and a handful of hazelnuts which Great Uncle Bulgaria loved.

"I wish it was my birthday," whispered Bungo, as the young Wombles tiptoed out. "I wonder how old Great Uncle Bulgaria is?"

But that, as every Womble knew, was a closely guarded secret. Only Great Uncle Bulgaria knew that . . . and of course, he was not telling!

W
W
TIMES
G.U.B.

WOMBLE WORDS

In winter, when bad weather keeps all the Wombles at home, Uncle Bulgaria tries to find something for everyone to do, so that no one gets restless. The young Wombles like games and puzzles, and so he devised this crossword puzzle for them to do. Some of the letters are already there to help you. Now you must use the picture clues to help you to fill in the rest of the letters.

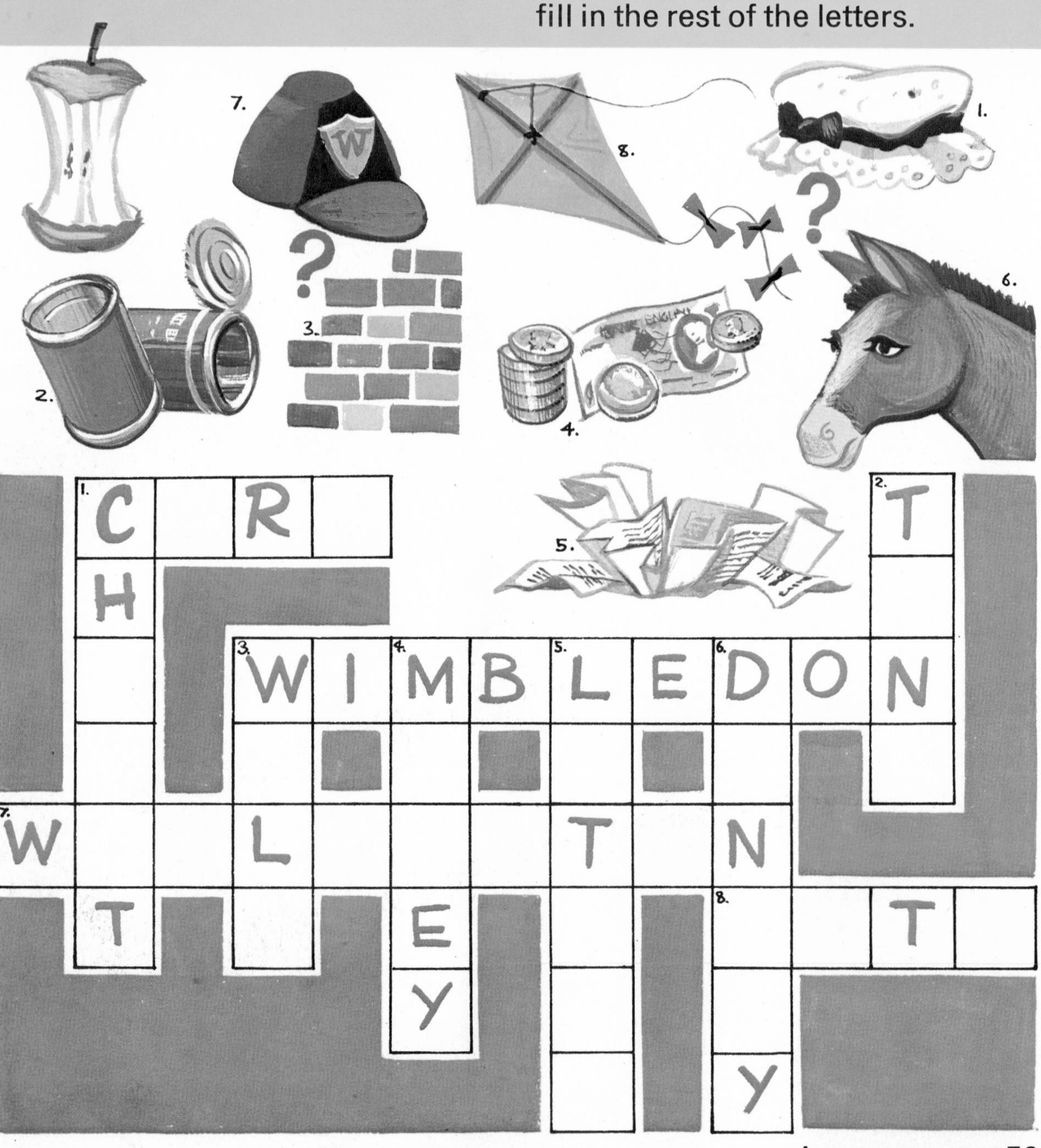

Answers on page 76

Madame Cholet and the Bracken Jam

Alderney and her great friend Shan-si were feeling very important, because Madame Cholet had told them that they could make Womble bracken jam all on their own.

"Just follow my cookery book carefully and all will be well," said Madame Cholet, "and while you are making the jam I shall be inventing a new pudding which I shall call Moss Sponge. Now off with you, but follow my directions EXACTLY!"

"I tell you what," said Alderney, who is just as bossy as Bungo, "first of all we'll pick the bracken and then we'll collect all the jam jars together. And when the jam is made you can draw pretty labels for the jars."

"Yes, please," said Shan-si, "I should like that."

But she spoke to an empty kitchen, for Alderney had already hurried off to the Workshop for two ENORMOUS tidy-bags.

Picking the bracken was a long job, but when Tomsk offered to help, Alderney waved him away, saying, "No. Thanks all the same. We're going to do everything ourselves. Come on Shan-si, there's another lovely patch of bracken over there."

According to the cookery book all the bracken leaves had to be stripped off the stems, then they had to be washed and weighed, and finally they had to be soaked overnight in ten pints of water.

"I tell you what," said Alderney, who was measuring out the water, "I think we could make more jam if we put in just a little more water."

"But Madame Cholet said we must follow directions EXACTLY," said Shan-si doubtfully.

"Yes, but think how pleased she'll be when she sees we've made extra jam," replied Alderney and poured out two extra pints of water.

The bracken leaves smelt very nice in the morning and, following the cookery book, Shan-si tied the chopped-up stems into a little bag and put it in with the leaves. Then Alderney put the bracken on the stove and heated it until it was just boiling.

In went the little bag, plus six pounds of clover sugar. After that all they had to do was to keep stirring the mixture. That was quite hard work too, but it was very exciting, because every minute the bracken smelt more and more like jam.

"Time's up," said Alderney, who had kept one eye on the clock. "Now we pour it into the jars."

Alderney had been quite right about one thing. The extra water she had added meant that they needed two extra jam jars.

"Won't Madame Cholet be pleased?" said Alderney, as she looked at the rows of jars which they had put to cool in the larder. "By tomorrow they will be full of lovely jelly bracken jam."

"*Um . . .* perhaps," said Shan-si doubtfully.

"Oh, come on, Old Worry Paws," said Alderney, "after all this hard work let's go and play Wombles and Ladders in the Playroom."

Very early next morning Alderney and Shan-si slipped out of bed and crept into the kitchen to look at their jam. But, early though it was, Madame Cholet was there before them, writing in her cookery book and looking rather worried.

"Please, what is the matter?" asked Shan-si in her soft little voice.

"It is my Moss Sponge. It is quite

good. I would even go so far as to say it is *very* good, and yet it lacks a certain something," replied Madame Cholet. "There is one little thing missing, but I do not know what it is exactly. However, let us now go and look at the jam. Yes?"

They went into the larder. There were the rows of jars looking like the very best bracken jam. Alderney felt so proud that she almost burst, but when Madame Cholet put a spoon into a jar all her proud feeling vanished. The jam hadn't set properly. It was quite thick, but it was runny at the same time and it slipped off the spoon like warm treacle.

"Oh . . . oh DEAR," said Alderney and Shan-si together.

"You have put in too much water," said Madame Cholet. "You did not follow my directions EXACTLY, did you?"

Miserably the two young Wombles shook their heads.

"It's all ruined," wailed Alderney, "and it's all my fault. It's more like sauce than jam. Oh dear, *oh dear,* OH DEAR!"

"One moment," said Madame Cholet. "Stop sniffing, Alderney. More like sauce than jam? But, of course, this is EXACTLY what I want."

Alderney and Shan-si stared wide-eyed at Madame Cholet, who smiled and wagged one finger at them as she said, "All cooks, even very good ones, make mistakes sometimes. But they turn those mistakes to their advantage . . . yes? This bracken sauce is just what my new Moss Sponge pudding needs. It will make all the difference. Shan-si, please draw some of your pretty labels for these jars."

"But what shall I write on them, please?" asked Shan-si.

"Bracken sauce, naturally. But next time you make JAM you will . . . "

"Follow your directions EXACTLY," said Alderney and Shan-si together.

"*Pre-cisely,*" said Madame Cholet.

WHAT DO YOU KNOW ABOUT THE WOMBLES?

Well, you know of course that they live on Wimbledon Common and help to keep it tidy. But if you can answer all these questions you are a real Wombles fan, and will be very welcome to call and see them any time you are passing their burrow.

1. When lorries forced the Wombles to seek a new home for a time, where did they go to live?

2. Which Womble welcomed them home wearing a battered yellow panama hat, a sacking apron and holding a flowerpot?

3. What is the car number of the Silver Womble?

4. Which Womble likes to do exercises before getting into bed?

5. Which Womble did Great Uncle Bulgaria take with him to America?

6. Who is the little Womble with a Chinese name who helps Madame Cholet and Alderney in the kitchen?

7. Who teaches the young Wombles in the Womblegarten?

8. Which Womble's name sounds like something to be worn in the rain?

9. Who says "Quel Dommage!" when things go wrong?

10. Madame Cholet created a new dish to celebrate Cousin Botany's return from Australia, and it was named in honour of another Womble who helped to make it.
What was the dish called?

Check your answers on page 76

MUSIC WHILE YOU WOMBLE

They call themselves the Litter Band, but if you look closely, you will probably see some familiar faces behind those instruments.

After the success of Tobermory's kazoos, the Wombles decided that they would like lots of different instruments so that they could form a band. As they brought the litter in from Wimbledon Common, Tobermory would put aside the likely-looking pieces, and then one day he shut himself in his workshop, and put a big sign on the door saying:

DO NOT DISTURB.

As they passed the door, the Wombles could hear strange noises coming from inside, and they waited eagerly for him to finish.

At last the door opened, and Tobermory appeared pushing a large box. "Now then," he said, "who wants what?" Suddenly, everyone seemed to be talking at once, but finally all the Wombles were given an instrument, and they settled down to practise.

You may like to form your own band, so here is what Tobermory used to make the instruments.

The milk bottles were filled with water to different levels, so that when they were tapped with a nail, they each made a different note.

The tambourine was made from an old tinfoil pie plate, with lots of bottle tops hanging from it, so it rattled when it was shaken.

The bongo drum was made from half a coconut, with a piece of inner tubing stretched across the top and attached with small nails.

Little Alderney's shakers were made from two washing-up liquid bottles, which were filled with dried peas, and fastened onto two sticks.

Finally, the 'triangle' was really a horseshoe dangling from a piece of string, and to make the note it was hit with a long nail.

MEET COUSIN BOTANY

Cousin Botany came all the way from Australia to pay the Wombles of Wimbledon a visit and to give Great Uncle Bulgaria a very important letter from the United States of America, which had arrived while the Wombles were living in Hyde Park.

Great Uncle Bulgaria and Tobermory remembered Botany as a very young Womble when he first came from Australia. Botany always had difficulty in telling people exactly what he meant, and sometimes this led to great difficulties.

He had arrived one morning at the Wimbledon Burrows because he had gone down to look at the docks in Sydney, and he had climbed on board a ship heading out to sea . . . and ended up for a time in England.

On his latest visit to England, worried by various world shortages, Botany had decided to try undersea farming on Queen's Mere but, unfortunately, since he told no one else of his ideas, Wellington and his friends ruined his experiments! *They* tried to find oil in Queen's Mere, and as a result disturbed all Botany's green under-water plants. He *was* annoyed! He actually threw down his ancient panama hat and stamped on it.

However, with Tobermory's help the project was started all over again, with all the Wombles helping. This time the underwater plants were put in tanks in the burrow.

When they were ready to eat Madame Cholet mixed the plants with various other ingredients and kneaded them together with a little grass flour. She made them into flat pieces and fried them carefully and a secret smile crossed her face as she thought up a very appropriate name for her new delicacy. Can you guess what it was . . . she called it a Botany Burger! Cousin Botany *was* pleased.

Picture Wombles

Here is a picture puzzle which gives you the name of some well-known Wombles:

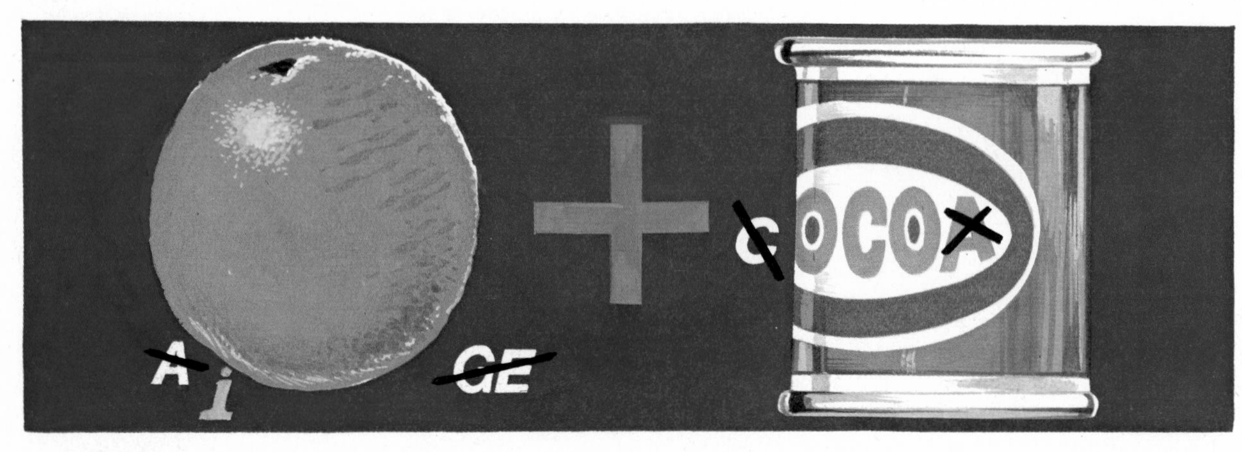

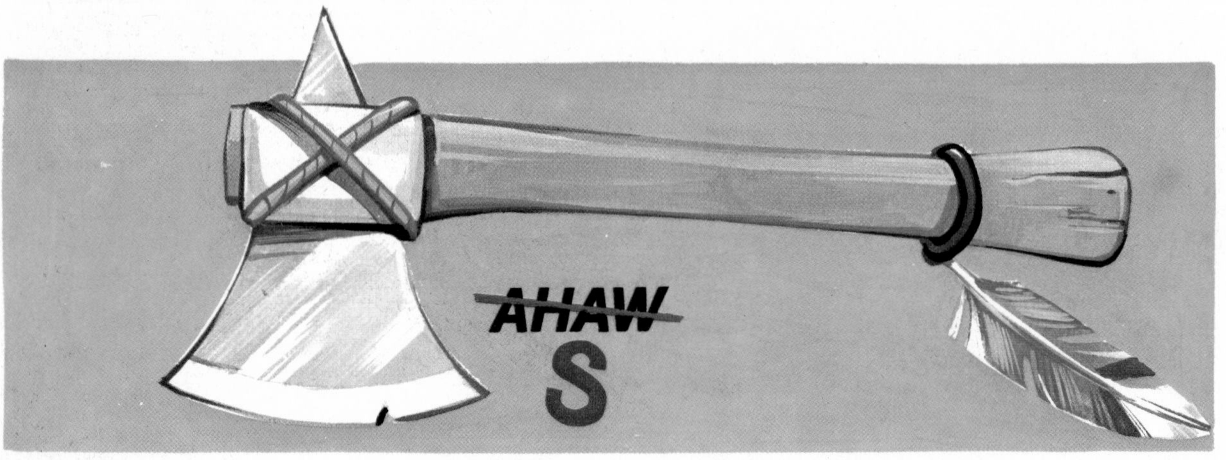

Answers on page 76

Wombles in Rhyme

Can you recognise these four well-known Wombles described in these rhymes?

1. Folks say I'm fat and lazy,
   But this I do deny,
   I love eating chocolate cake,
   "You're so greedy!" the others cry.
   WHO AM I?

2. I'm busy in my workshop,
   Making lots of things,
   Like my wonderful Silver Womble,
   Which travels as if on wings.
   WHO AM I?

3. I am the Nightwatch Womble,
   The tallest of them all,
   And I am very clever
   With a golf club and a ball.
   WHO AM I?

4. It is now many years,
   Since I left my native shores,
   To live in the United States,
   In a great park out of doors.
   WHO AM I?

Check your answers on page 76

CAPTAIN BUNGO and the SS WOMBLE

"Look what I've found," said Bungo, bustling into the burrow in his usual bossy way.

"What?" asked Orinoco, who was wondering if there was time for twenty winks before supper.

"It's a book all about boats. I've always wanted to go on a boat. I think I'd make a very good water Womble, and I bet I'd never be sea-sick," replied Bungo.

"Excuse me," said Wellington in his quiet way, "but it's not a book, you know. It's what's called a brochure, and it's not about boats, but SHIPS. It's telling Human Beings about winter cruises on the Union Castle Line and . . ."

"Boats, ships, brochures, books, who cares," interrupted Bungo, "it's all the same really. Anyway I vote we build our own boat-ship and sail

Broch-whatever-it-is. Come on, Orinoco, you'll like sailing. It says here that you can laze about and sunbathe all day on these boats."

Orinoco brightened up a bit on hearing this and, as there was no longer time for twenty winks he followed his two friends into the back Workshop where Tobermory stored all kinds of useful bits and pieces which had been thrown away or dumped by Human Beings.

The three young Wombles spent some time sorting through the neatly stacked mounds of rubbish, each one burrowing away in his own part of the Workshop, as he looked for exactly what he felt would make a good waterproof boat. Wellington made a pile of bits of old bicycles. Bungo discovered the remains of an old dinghy and as for Orinoco all he came up with was a small wooden door which had GARDEN SHED painted on it.

"We'll never make a boat out of this lot," said Bungo in a very cross voice.

it on the Queen's Mere. Bags I be the Captain and we'll call it . . . what *shall* we call it?"

"*Um,* the ss *Womble*. The 'ss' stands for sailing ship. At least I think it does," said Wellington a shade doubtfully. "But how can we build a ship, Bungo? Ships are ENORMOUS."

"We'll build just a little one, and we'll copy the pictures in this

"Yes, we will," argued Wellington. "I've got a lot of ideas already. Haven't you, Orinoco?"

But Orinoco didn't reply. He was only thinking about his supper.

Although it was Wellington who had all the ideas, Bungo soon took charge of everything, and for the next few days he enjoyed himself a great deal as he told the others what to do.

"I bet we're the first Womble shipwrights ever," he said happily as the ss Womble began to take shape.

"Ship-*wrongs'*d be nearer the mark," muttered Wellington. "It'll never float, Bungo. I'm sure it won't."

"Yes, it will. Put another patch on here, Orinoco, and Wellington, you'd better get some more rope for tying on the – er – the boat deck."

Great Uncle Bulgaria and Tobermory tiptoed in late one evening to look at the ss *Womble* after everybody else was in bed asleep and, in some cases, snoring.

"My word! My goodness me! *Ho-HUM,"* said Great Uncle Bulgaria, "well, well, WELL. It doesn't look at all like the graceful, elegant ships of the Union Castle Line. It is a – a – – a most remarkable shape. What do you think, Tobermory?"

"It'll sink," said Tobermory, *"tck tck tck."*

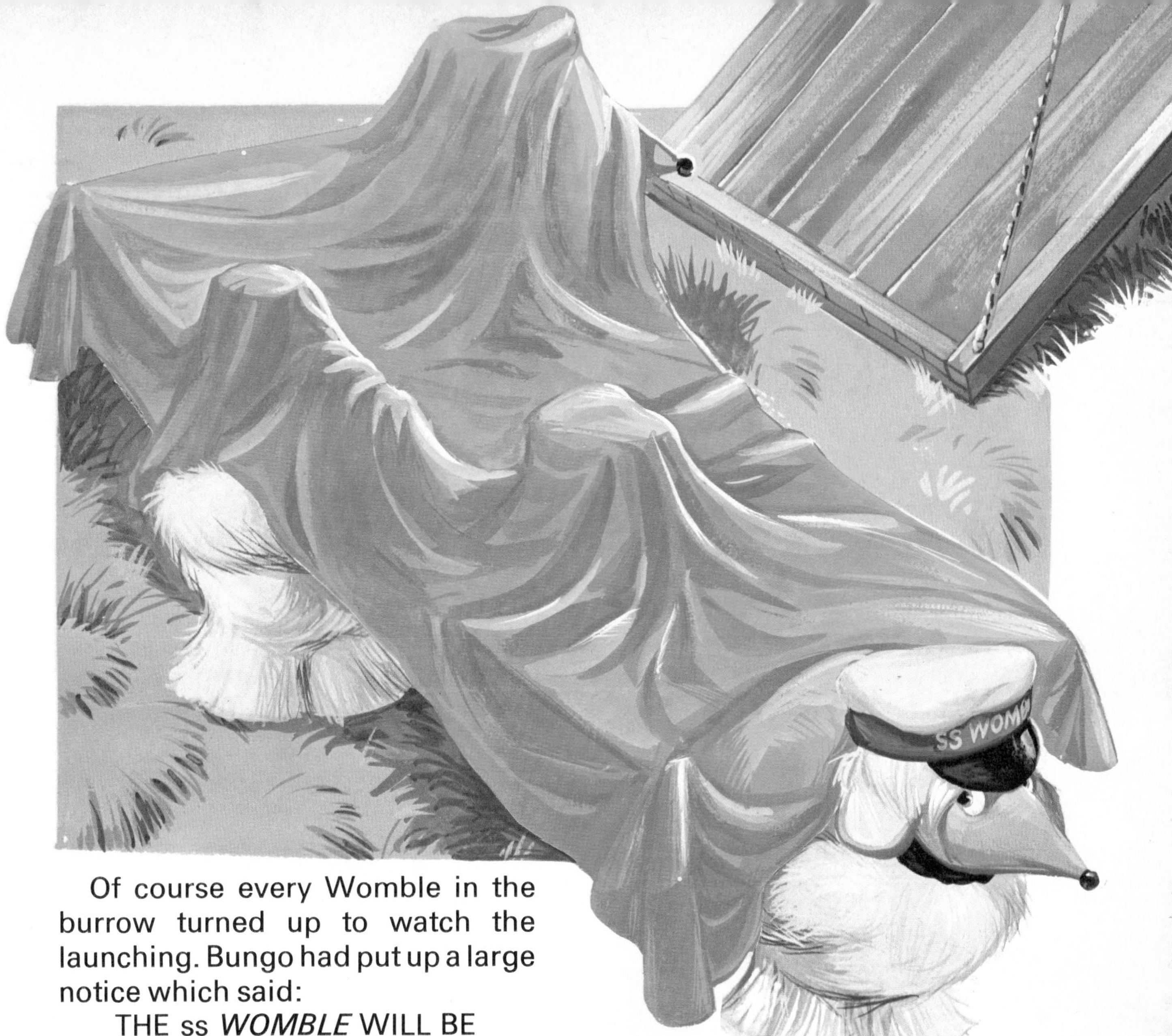

Of course every Womble in the burrow turned up to watch the launching. Bungo had put up a large notice which said:

THE ss *WOMBLE* WILL BE LUNCHED

(Miss Adelaide had added an 'A' up above the L and the U, but it still looked like LUNCHED)

AT 5.30 EXACTLY.

There was a cheer as Bungo, wearing a cap with ss *Womble* on it, came out of the Workshop carrying one end of the boat. The boat itself was covered in an old tablecloth so that Wellington, who was carrying the middle part on his shoulders, and Orinoco, who was carrying the end on his shoulders, were invisible apart from their back paws, as the tablecloth covered the rest of them. However, there were cries of, "Go it, Wellington", "Hooray for Orinoco", as they lurched out of the burrow and towards Queen's Mere.

When they reached the water Tomsk blew a blast on a home-made bugle, which made Great Uncle Bulgaria's fur stand on end because it was rather a shrill sort of sound, and then Madame Cholet stepped forward with a carton of blackberry juice and said: "I name

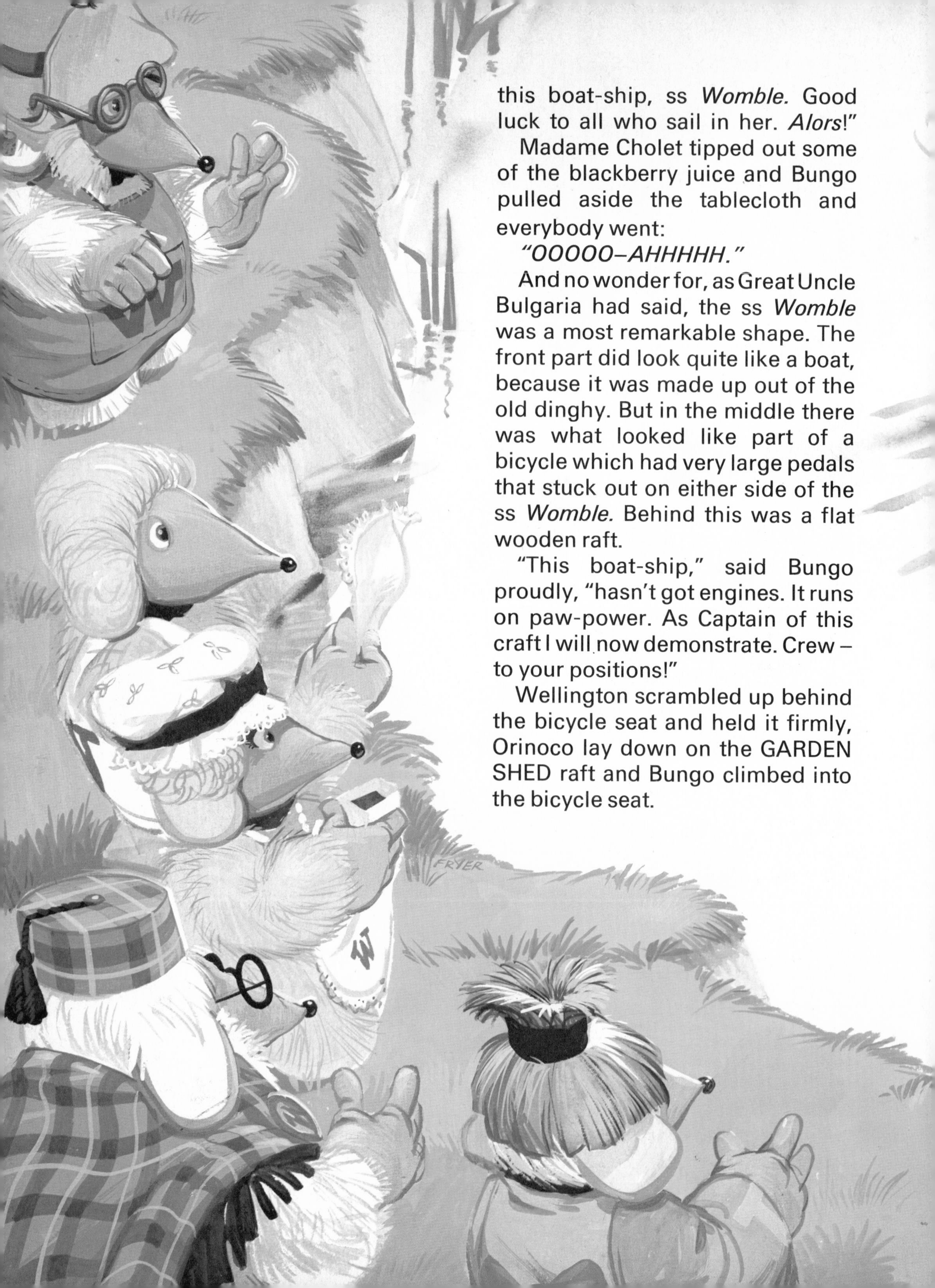

this boat-ship, ss *Womble.* Good luck to all who sail in her. *Alors*!"

Madame Cholet tipped out some of the blackberry juice and Bungo pulled aside the tablecloth and everybody went:

"OOOOO–AHHHHH."

And no wonder for, as Great Uncle Bulgaria had said, the ss *Womble* was a most remarkable shape. The front part did look quite like a boat, because it was made up out of the old dinghy. But in the middle there was what looked like part of a bicycle which had very large pedals that stuck out on either side of the ss *Womble.* Behind this was a flat wooden raft.

"This boat-ship," said Bungo proudly, "hasn't got engines. It runs on paw-power. As Captain of this craft I will now demonstrate. Crew – to your positions!"

Wellington scrambled up behind the bicycle seat and held it firmly, Orinoco lay down on the GARDEN SHED raft and Bungo climbed into the bicycle seat.

All the Wombles on the bank stopped shuffling and talking and laughing and Bungo began to pedal as fast as he could go. The ss *Womble* surged into the water and started to churn across Queen's Mere.

It was a most remarkable sight, and after a few moments Great Uncle Bulgaria called out: "Well done! Hooray! Three cheers for Captain Bungo . . ."

But before the three cheers were finished something very strange happened. The ss *Womble* began to sink. It went down quite slowly, inch by inch, and no matter how fast Bungo pedalled he couldn't stop it.

Everybody on shore held their breath and crossed their fingers, but it didn't do any good. Nothing could save the ss *Womble.* The only one who wasn't worried was Orinoco who, quite worn out, had gone fast asleep with his paws crossed on his fat little tummy and a happy smile on his face. The ropes came undone and Orinoco drifted contentedly away on his 'sun deck'.

"Glug, glug, glug," said Wellington and Captain Bungo as the ss *Womble* vanished under the water.

Nobody on the bank said anything until they re-appeared a few moments later.

"I tell you what," said Bungo, bobbing up with Wellington right beside him, "I'm not very keen on boat-ships really. I think I'll invent something else instead."

"And what's THAT?" asked Great Uncle Bulgaria and Tobermory in one voice.

"The first ever Womble submarine," announced Bungo. "I say, where's Orinoco gone?"

The only answer was a deep *"ZZZZZ"*.

For Orinoco was fast asleep having a nice FIFTY winks on the sun deck (GARDEN SHED DOOR) of the late, sunk and unlamented ss *WOMBLE.*

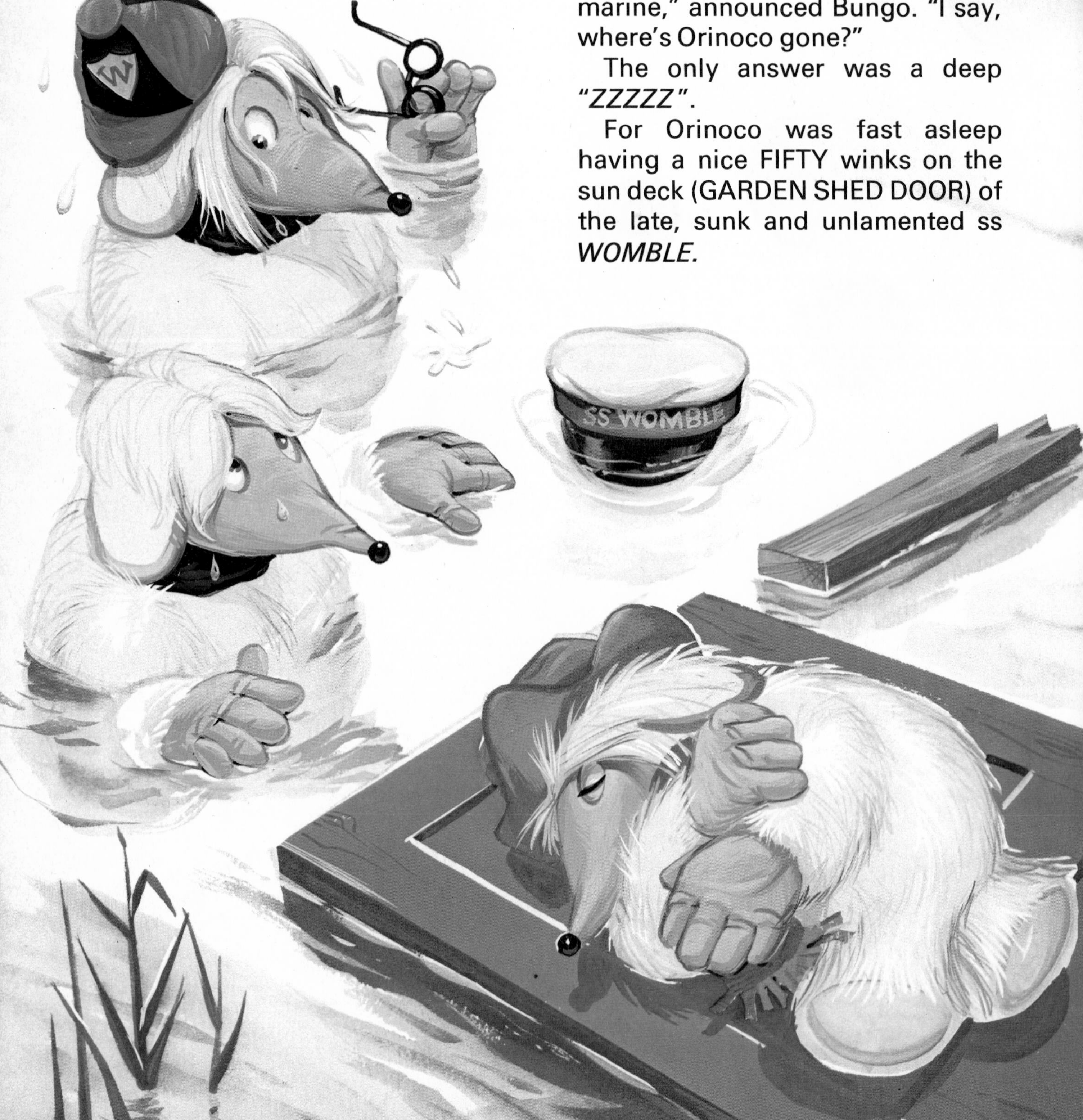

WELLINGTON WANTS TO KNOW...

THE SNOW WOMBLE

One snowy day the Wombles made a Snow Womble, and now Wellington wants to know:

1. To whom does the Snow Womble's shawl belong?
2. Who lent the Snow Womble his golf club?
3. Who lent the Snow Womble his floppy hat?
4. Who usually has the screwdriver which is behind his ear?

PICTURE NAMES

Wellington wants to know whose names are spelt out in these pictures.

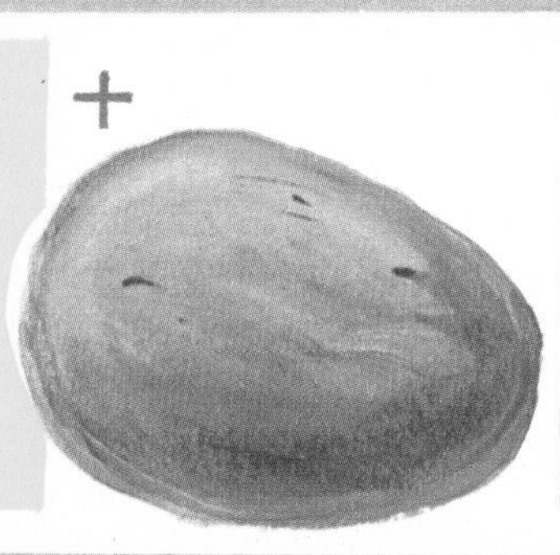

NAME THE TREE

Wellington wants to know which tree this fruit and flower comes from:

Check your answers on page 76

Madame Cholet's PARTY

The Wombles get very, very hungry when they are out hunting litter, and Madame Cholet always has a lovely dinner ready for them when they get home.

Often the Wombles have a big party. There is lots to eat and lots to drink. Madame Cholet usually makes all the sandwiches and cakes, but sometimes the other Wombles help her to make some extra special treats. See if you can make some Womble specials for your party.

Great Uncle Bulgaria's Favourite Crispy Sandwiches

You will need:

8 slices of buttered bread
3 tablespoons of chutney or pickle
$^{1}/_{2}$lb cheese, cut in slices or grated.
3 beaten eggs
3 ounces corn flakes
(turn the oven onto gas number 6 or electricity 400°F)

How you make them:

1 Spread four slices of the buttered bread with the chutney.
2 Top with slices of cheese and sandwich with the remaining bread.
3 Cut off the crusts and cut each sandwich into two triangles.
4 Dip each triangle in the beaten egg so it is covered completely.
5 Crush the cornflakes.
6 Coat the sandwiches in the cornflakes and place them on a greased baking tray.
7 Put them in the hot oven for 10 minutes, or until they are crisp.

A Womble Special is ready for serving.

Tobermory loves ice cream and lemonade, and with these sodas he can have them both together!

You will need:

1 family sized brick of vanilla ice cream
1 large bottle of lemonade
1 apple, orange, and a jar of cocktail cherries
cocktail sticks
straws
tall glasses

How to make them:

1 Take as many tall glasses as you have guests and fill them $\frac{3}{4}$ full with the lemonade.
2 Place a scoop of ice cream in each glass.
3 Decorate some with slices of apple, and others with two cherries and a slice of orange on a cocktail stick.
4 Pop two straws in each glass and serve at once.

ORINOCO'S ROWBOAT

You will need:

1 swiss roll
1 family block of icecream
8 whole strawberries
some fruity-flavoured syrup
8 wooden or plastic icecream spoons

How you make it:

1 Cut the swiss roll into nine slices and the icecream into eight slices.
2 Arrange them alternately down a long oval dish.
3 Put a strawberry on each slice of icecream.
4 Pour some fruity-flavoured syrup over the strawberry-men and the boat.
5 Put four icecream spoons on each side of the boat, sticking them into the icecream to make oars.
Serve at once.

TOMSK'S ORANGY CRISPS

After a good round of golf Tomsk loves orangy crisps at teatime.

You will need:

1 ounce margarine or butter
1 ounce caster sugar
3 tablespoons Tate and Lyle orange syrup
3 ounces rice crispies

How you make them:

1 Melt together the margarine, sugar and orange syrup over a low heat until they are dissolved.
2 Turn up the heat and boil them for one minute, stirring all the time (you can ask an adult to help you with this).
3 Stir in the rice crispies and mix well with a wooden spoon.
4 Put the mixture into a greased tin about 7 inches by 7 inches.
5 Press it down well, but don't break too many of the crispies.
6 Leave it to stand in a cool place for half an hour.
7 Cut it into squares.

The Wandering Wombles

As you can see from the maps four well-known Wombles have gone visiting, but where do they each really live?

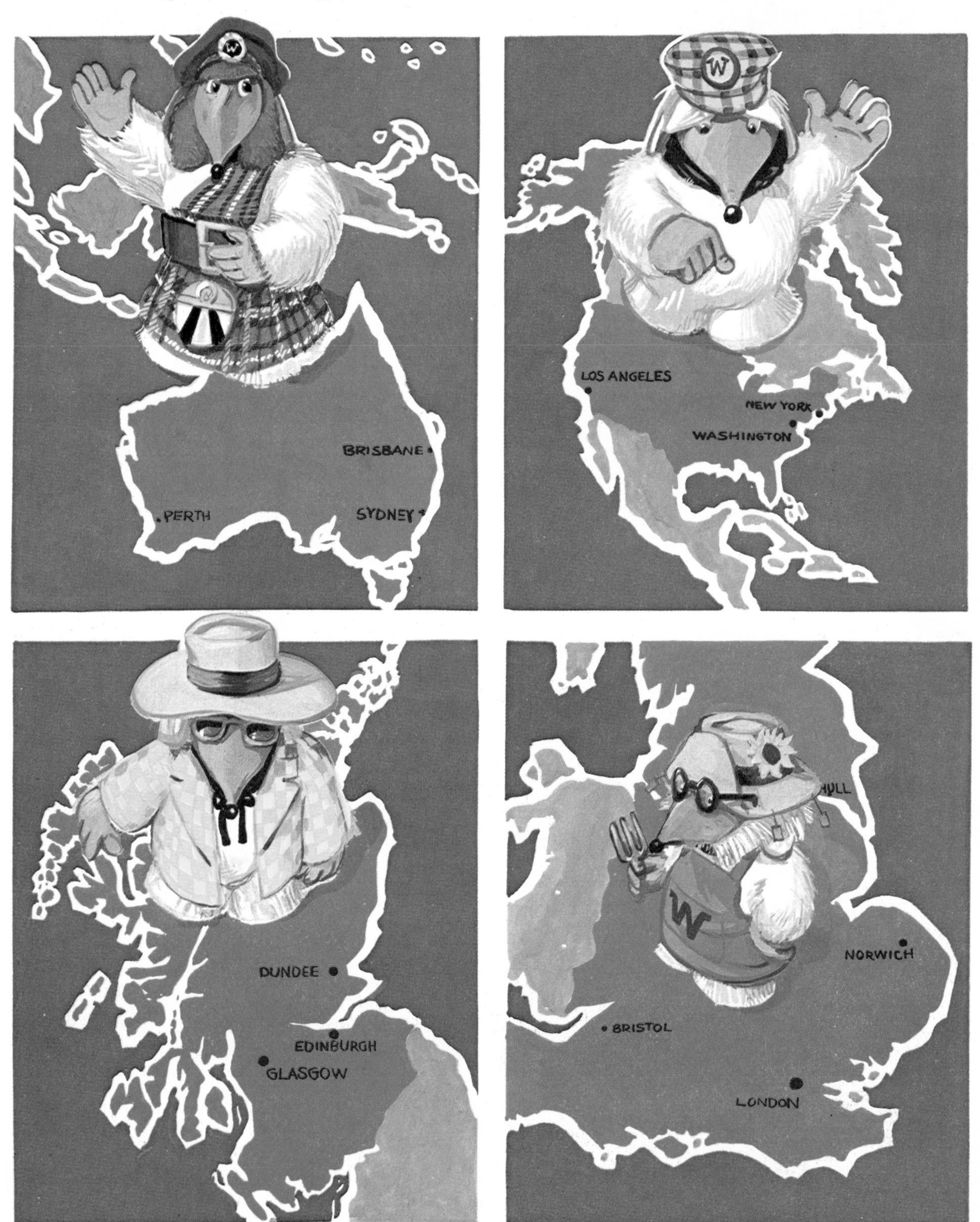

Check your answers on page 76

ORINOCO catches a cold.

Orinoco had a really awful cold. Great Uncle Bulgaria said that he had probably got it from having a "nice forty winks" in a damp blackberry bush.

"Nonsense, Bulgaria," said Madame Cholet, "you are being very unkind. Poor little Orinoco is not at all well. I shall take him some hot acorn juice and . . ."

The rest of Madame Cholet's words were drowned by the most dreadful roaring-shouting-exploding noise: "EEE-RUMPH". It was so violent it made all the doors in the burrow rattle.

"What was *that*?" demanded Great Uncle Bulgaria, holding onto the papers on his desk as they were being blown about.

"That," replied Madame Cholet, "is poor little Orinoco sneezing. He always shouts when he sneezes. I don't know why, but it does show just how bad his cold is."

"Ho-hum," said Great Uncle Bulgaria, who had started to think about other, rather more important things. One of which was that the hand on his barometer had moved right round from 'Fair' to 'Fog' during the last half-hour.

There hadn't been a bad fog in London for years and years, but the weather had been very odd recently, changing from 'Quite Warm' to 'Really Chilly' all in the same day.

"Very worrying!" muttered Great Uncle Bulgaria. "I hope all the young Wombles who are on tidying-up work are back in the burrow by now or they might get lost."

Off he went to the front door where he became even more worried as he saw that none of the working Wombles had ticked off their names in the Work Book. That meant they were all still out on the Common.

"Dear, dear, dear!" said Great Uncle Bulgaria, and he opened the front door.

Behind him there was another enormously loud, "EEE-RUMPH", but the old Womble hardly noticed it, for swirling before him were thick, twirling clouds of fog. He could hardly see a yard ahead of his nose.

"Tck tck tck," muttered Great Uncle Bulgaria, taking off his spectacles and wiping them and then blowing his nose, for the fog smelt rather nasty.

"I hope you haven't caught young Orinoco's cold," said Tobermory, who had just come out of his Workshop with a large lantern in one paw.

"No, no, it's this dratted fog," replied the old Womble. "What's that lantern for, Tobermory?"

"It's what you might call a 'homing beacon'. I'm going to put it on the roof of the burrow so that the light will help the young working Wombles to find their way home. My word, Bulgaria, we haven't had a real pea soup fog like this in years. Here, you hold the lantern while I climb up onto the roof."

"Do you think it'll work?" asked Great Uncle Bulgaria doubtfully.

"It'll *have* to work," replied Tobermory. "We haven't had any need for

a fog beacon for so long that it was all I could find in a hurry. Of course if I'd have had some warning the weather was going to change I might have been able to invent something better." And Tobermory looked accusingly at Great Uncle Bulgaria.

"It's no good blaming me," said the old Womble crossly, "the barometer didn't give me any warning at all. Oh dear, oh dear, Tobermory, big though it is, that lantern doesn't give much light, does it?"

The two Wombles stared up at the roof of the burrow where the lantern was giving out a cloudy yellow glow. When the fog thinned out for a second or two the light was quite strong, but the trouble was that the moment the fog grew thicker the lantern dimmed right down.

There was a moment's silence while the two Wombles peered anxiously at the lantern and then turned and gazed into the swirling, twirling fog. Somewhere out there in the darkness were Bungo, Wellington and Tomsk, who were probably quite lost, a little bit scared, and certainly very hungry.

Suddenly the silence was shattered.

"EEE-RUMPH" bellowed Orinoco, producing the sneeze of a lifetime. It made Tobermory's bowler hat fall onto his nose and it blew Great Uncle Bulgaria's shawl almost off his shoulders.

"Stupid young Womble," muttered Tobermory, "making all that row, why . . . OH! That's it. That's the answer."

"What is? Do stop talking through your hat, Tobermory."

"Sorry," said Tobermory putting his hat straight. "Listen, Bulgaria, I think I've got the answer to our little problem of fog-bound Wombles. It's this . . ." and Tobermory began to talk faster and faster while Great Uncle Bulgaria's eyes grew round as buttons as he listened.

At the finish he said, "I do believe you're right, Tobermory. Call Orinoco IMMEDIATELY."

Out on the Common, Tomsk, Wellington and Bungo were all huddled together, standing back to back as they tried to make out where they were.

"It's funny how easy it is to get lost," said Wellington, "and I thought I knew the Common like the back of my paw. I think the burrow is THAT way." And he pointed.

"No, it isn't, it's that way," said Bungo, pointing.

"It's not. It's this way," said Tomsk.

The three young Wombles looked at each other in dismay. They were hopelessly lost. They were tired, they were a bit scared, and they were very, very hungry.

"What shall we do?" whispered Wellington, "we can't stay out here all night and . . ."

He stopped speaking as, echoing through the fog, came a faint, but familiar sound.

"EEEE-RUMPH!"

"It's Orinoco," said Bungo, "and because of his cold he's home safe and sound. All we have to do is to follow the sound of his sneezing. It came from over there. Everybody join paws and follow me. Good old Orinoco."

The sneezes came at irregular intervals, but they grew louder and louder until at last the three young Wombles saw the faint light of the lantern on top of the burrow. And then they heard the cross, but very welcoming sound of Great Uncle Bulgaria saying, "Stupid young Wombles, getting lost on your own Common. Well come in, come in and shut the door behind you. Tomsk, get that beacon thing, turn it off and bring it inside. Dear me, you're more trouble than you're worth, but welcome home. Supper's ready."

"I tell you what," said Bungo, when everybody was sitting nice and warm and cosy in the kitchen, "I think Orinoco should have two helpings of *everything* for guiding us home on his 'Sneezing Beacon'."

"It'z very kind of you," said Orinoco, "to zuggest it. But becauzze of my cold, I can't zmell any food. Zo I'm not all that hungry. Zorry."

"Poor little Orinoco," said Madame Cholet, "off you go to bed and I will bring you some hot acorn juice."

Everybody went "*tck tck tck*" as Orinoco, sniffing and snuffling, made for the door. He stopped for a moment and all the other Wombles put their paws over their ears and waited.

"EEEE-RUMPH," said Orinoco.

Count with the Wombles

For a special winter treat, Great Uncle Bulgaria and Tobermory took the Wombles down to Queen's Mere for a winter picnic. They wrapped up warmly, and Madame Cholet made lots of hot drinks and delicious food to eat, and they all had lots of fun skating on the mere which had frozen over.

Here is a picture of the Wombles enjoying themselves. Look carefully and then answer these questions:

1. How many Wombles are wearing scarves?
2. How many Wombles are carrying muffs?
3. How many Wombles are drinking blackcurrant juice?
4. How many Wombles are eating hot potatoes?
5. How many Wombles are skating?
6. How many Wombles are wearing spectacles?

Check your answers on page 76

Wellington's Word Game

As you know, Wellington Womble is the studious one, always reading and trying to discover new facts. Well one day, as he was writing his name in his exercise book, it occurred to him that it was possible to make other words from the letters by rearranging them.

He managed to make fifty-four words, all of three letters or more, and only using the letters in his name. Why not see if you can beat his total?

Here are some to start you off, and then it's up to you. WENT, TOWN, LINE, NOT . . .

BE A WOMBLE TOO!

When you're out in town or country,
Out in woodland, field or road,
Out walking or on a picnic,
Please remember the litter code.

Never, never leave sweet papers,
Or bags or open tins,
In field or street or parkland,
Just look out for the litter bins.

The Wombles clear Wimbledon Common,
But they can't always be around.
So children, you start Wombling too,
And keep all litter off the ground.

FULL of BEANS!

Bean-bags are great fun for throwing-type games, so here is one for you to make in the shape of your favourite Womble.

You will need:

Material
Scraps of felt
Scissors
Glue
Needle, pins and thread
Dried peas, beans or rice.

Before you can start your bean-bag, you must make a pattern by tracing the drawing of a Womble onto some greaseproof paper, and cutting it out.

Using this pattern, cut two Womble shapes from your material, remembering to leave about ½" all the way round as a seam allowance, and pin them together.

Sew neatly round the shape, leaving a couple of inches at the top so that you can fill it, and turn it through so that all the raw edges are on the inside. Fill with the dried peas, beans or rice, and close up the gap by oversewing the edges.

Now trace off the shape of the Womble's face, and cut this out in your felt. Stick it in place, and either draw on the eyes and nose with a felt pen, or cut them out in different felt and stick them on.

Your bean-bag Womble is now finished, and ready for all the games you will want to invent for it. If you made a few, perhaps you could learn to juggle with them, but whatever you do, you are sure to have lots of fun.

Cousin Botany Womble and the Kangaroo

Cousin Botany is a very shy, very old Womble who lives in the Wimbledon Common burrow, but who keeps himself to himself. This isn't because he doesn't like the other Wombles; it's just that he lives in a world of his own. And his particular world is gardening. Just as Madame Cholet is probably the best Womble cook in the whole world, so Cousin Botany is probably the best Womble gardener. He has what the other Wombles call 'green paws'.

Now one dark evening Wellington was tidying up quite close to where Cousin Botany has his little, hidden greenhouses. Wellington was tiptoeing past as quietly as he could so as not to disturb Cousin Botany when suddenly, without any warning, there was a *'flip-flap-flop'* sound right beside him.

Wellington was so startled that he almost jumped out of his fur, for quite a large animal was bounding straight towards him. Wellington stood stock still and the animal sprang right over his head, missed the greenhouses by a whisker and vanished.

"*EEeeeee*!" said Wellington and dropped his tidy-bag with a clatter.

"Who's that?" said the slow, gruff voice of Cousin Botany from the shadows.

"Me, Wellington. Sorry. But there was this ENORMOUS wild animal and it sprang at me. Oh dear."

"Wild animal? Oh my word, young Womble, that was just a hare. A big rabbit, like. They come on the Common from time to time, but where they come *from* and where they go *to* I can't tell. And as for springing at you, it wouldn't hurt a sparrow, that hare wouldn't. *Tck tck tck,* and call that jumping! Why, I could tell of animals ten times the size of that hare that really *do* jump. One of 'em took me hat off me once. *Heh, heh, heh.*"

"What – what sort of animal?" Wellington asked nervously. He'd had quite a fright and it was rather a wild, dark evening.

"Come inside do, then," said Cousin Botany, who knew a scared

young Womble when he saw one. "You can help me pot out my sweet-corn while I tell you."

The little greenhouses smelt nice and homely and Wellington stopped twitching as old Cousin Botany gave him a trowel and some pots and then went on in his slow way.

" 'Twas a long while ago, when I was a young Womble myself in Australia, that I set off to pay a call on Great Aunt Murrumbidgee Womble. Away I went with my 'tucker' – that's food all done up in a spotted handkerchief tied to the end of a stick. It was a long journey of hundreds of miles. But in those days there weren't very many Human Beings in Australia, so I could use the main tracks without fear of meeting them. There were all kinds of animals along the way. Dingoes, wild dogs they are and nasty tempers they've got, so I kept well clear of them; koala bears, living high up in their blue gum trees. Now they're a nice kind of creature, gentle and polite. So were the wallabies. And there were birds of all kinds like the kookaburra and the lyre bird with his lovely tail.

"So it happens that about my third or fourth day on the track I was plodding along, not thinking of anything much, when suddenly there's this *thud thud thud* sound coming up behind me. Right by a thorn tree I was, so naturally, being a sensible young Womble, I took cover. The *thud thud thud* grew louder and louder and LOUDER. The ground seemed to shake with the noise of it. Suddenly there was a crashing noise, then a groan . . . and then silence. So being inquisitive like all Wombles, I crept out to have a look. And there before me in the sunlight was a truly ENORMOUS animal flat on its side and not breathing. It had hit its head on a thorn tree and it

looked as if it was done for, poor thing. Ten feet from head to tail it was."

"Ten feet LONG," breathed Wellington. "That really is enormous."

"So never having seen the like before, I took off my bush-wacker hat and waved it over it. Nothing happened. So I put my hat on its head to protect it from the sun, which was something very fierce, and I started to undo my tucker bag to see if there was anything in it which would help this animal. All of a sudden it came alive again. It sat up and looked at me and then it got to its back paws and it jumped right

to go fuzzy in front of my eyes. I couldn't see straight no more. I could hardly put one paw before the other until at last I fell flat on my nose and just lay there.

"Then, very softly, I heard a *thud thud thud* and I felt myself being lifted up and carried and a while after that somebody was giving me a nice cool drink and I heard voices. There was a lovely, familiar smell too. The smell of a friendly Womble burrow. I opened my eyes and there was Great Aunt Murrumbidgee smiling from ear to ear, with all her Wombles behind her, such as Cousins Brisbane and Burke and young Eucla as well as Cairns and Perth. And behind them, and five times their size was . . ."

"Who?"

over my head and over the thorn bushes too and it vanished.

"Now the sun in that part of Australia is very, very, VERY hot. And there was me with no hat. And although I'd nice thick fur it didn't stop the sun from striking on my head. After a bit I began to feel very sick and strange, and I was still a long way from Great Aunt Murrumbidgee's burrow. In fact, young Womble, I started to think I was done for. I don't know how many hours I walked, and then staggered, and after a while everything seemed

"Why, this kangaroo. Funny sort of animal he was, especially as he was still wearing my hat! It seems as if once he'd come to his proper senses again, after knocking himself out on the thorn bush, he'd thought things over and gone looking for help. He'd got kangaroos all over Australia searching for Wombles to come to my aid. I shook his paw and he shook mine, because one good turn always deserves another. And we had a little talk, and the result of it all was that I let him keep my hat."

"And what happened then?" asked Wellington.

"The kangaroo went leaping off to join his family and I had a very nice holiday with my Womble relations.

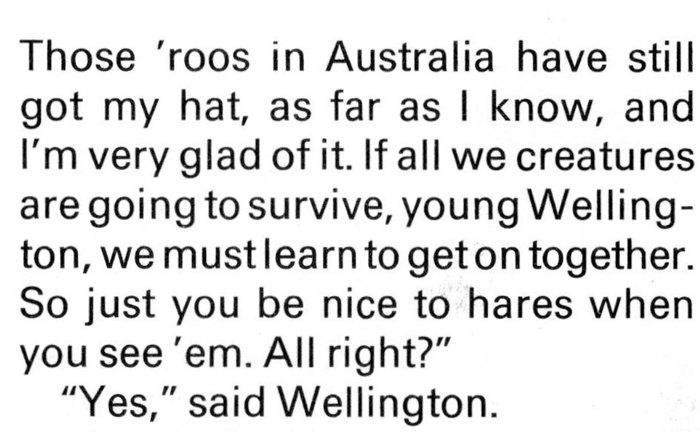

Those 'roos in Australia have still got my hat, as far as I know, and I'm very glad of it. If all we creatures are going to survive, young Wellington, we must learn to get on together. So just you be nice to hares when you see 'em. All right?"

"Yes," said Wellington.

"Good-oh," said Cousin Botany, potting out the rest of the sweetcorn. "Off you go, young Wellington, and ask Madame Cholet to keep some tucker for me."

"Good-oh," said Wellington, "yes I *will,* Cousin Botany."

Christmas Silhouettes

One Christmas Eve Bungo and Wellington crept downstairs into the kitchen to take a look at some of the Christmas surprises Madam Cholet had prepared. Of course, it was rather naughty of them, and it was very dark too, so they could only see the silhouettes. But they still managed to know what they were. Can you say what the shadows remind you of?

Check your answers on page 76

Before the very young Wombles become important enough to choose a name for themselves out of Great Uncle Bulgaria's atlas and be given an important job in the burrow, they stay each day in the Womblegarten where Miss Adelaide teaches them everything a good young Womble should know.

She teaches sums and spelling, and she is always pleased when someone finds clean notepaper or pens and pencils on the Common, because her one fear is that there will one day be a shortage and lessons will have to stop.

She was therefore extremely delighted when Wellington and Shansi invented some plastic slates which could be used over and over again. Shansi had been top of the Womblegarten painting class and she had created a special Womble Willow Pattern which she painted on lots of cups, saucers and plates. Miss Adelaide finally put Shansi, the little Womble with the Chinese place name, in charge of the Paw-craft Class.

Probably because they have all been taught by Miss Adelaide, most of the Wombles are rather afraid of her, even Tobermory does not like to upset her because she can be very stern when things are not right!

But she knows that young Wombles must play sometimes, and she indulgently allows them to play an exciting game of 'Wombles and Ladders'.

A BUSY LITTLE WOMBLE

If you take the first letter from each picture it will make up the name of the busy little Womble who picked up all these objects one day on Wimbledon Common.

Check your answers on page 76

I spy something beginning with 'W'...

If there's one thing Bungo likes, when he's finished his jobs of course, it's a good game of 'I Spy'. In fact, he even likes it so much that he often plays it when he's on his own.

So, especially for Bungo, and you, if you like playing 'I Spy', here's a page for you to look at very closely....

Because if you look closely you'll find five animals hidden here whose names begin with 'W' and you might find one more thing too . . . whose name begins with 'W'.

Turn to page 76 for your answers

TOMSK MEETS AN OLD FRIEND.

It had snowed and snowed, so that Wimbledon Common looked as if it was covered with an enormous white fluffy blanket. All the young Wombles enjoyed themselves very much indeed, having snowball fights and sliding up and down Queen's Mere which was almost a block of solid ice. Because it was so cold very few human beings were out on the Common, which meant that there was hardly any rubbish to be collected.

"It's all very well for them," said Great Uncle Bulgaria, standing at the doorway of the burrow and

blowing on his fingers, "but I must say I shall be glad when the snow goes. Never did like snow, I'm too old to try and walk through it, and I do miss my little walks."

Very early the next morning, when it was still half dark, Tomsk went out on his home-made skis to have some exercise before breakfast. He was *shushing* along over the snow when, to his astonishment, he saw *another Womble coming towards him!* Now Tomsk knew very well that he'd left everybody else tucked up, and in some cases, snoring, in the burrow.

"I'm dreaming," muttered Tomsk, and pinched himself.

But the strange Womble refused to vanish and, what was more, the other Womble was *shushing* over the snow even faster and better than Tomsk had ever managed to do.

Tomsk stood still and watched with his eyes as round as marbles.

He felt a little bit scared, and a little bit excited . . . and then suddenly the strange Womble lifted up one paw and shouted, "Hello, Tomsk, old friend, it is me, Omsk!"

"Omsk!" exclaimed Tomsk,

Everybody was, and like Tomsk they were very glad to see Omsk again. They had met him during the time when the Wimbledon burrow was being repaired and they had all had to go and live in the old burrow in Hyde Park for a while.

"Omsk Womble, what are you doing here? I thought you were living in the burrow under Hyde Park."

"So I am," replied Omsk, *shushing* up alongside Tomsk and shaking his paw so hard that Tomsk nearly fell over. "With all the other Hyde Park Wombles, who send their greetings, by the way. But with all of London covered in snow I thought I'd ski over to see my Wimbledon cousins. I hope you don't mind?"

"Course not. Jolly pleased," replied Tomsk, "I say, what a smashing surprise. Come inside. Everybody'll be ASTONISHED."

Omsk was as big as Tomsk, and even better at all winter sports, and he was soon teaching Wellington how to do 'figures of eight' on Queen's Mere, and Bungo how to toboggan on his fat little stomach... and he even got Orinoco to try ski-jumping. So all the young Wombles enjoyed themselves even more than usual.

But Omsk, who perhaps because he was a visiting Womble noticed things that the others didn't, realised that Great Uncle Bulgaria was a bit out of sorts.

"Excuse me," said Omsk, in his rumbling voice, "but do you not like the snow, Great Uncle Bulgaria?"

"It's all right in its way, young Womble, but between you and me and the front door, I do miss my little walks. You can't expect a Womble of my age to trudge through snow, now can you?"

"Ah," said Omsk, "but in Russia and Finland and the Scandinavian countries where there is much snow, the older Wombles travel about by sledski. No?"

"No, I mean yes," said Great Uncle Bulgaria, who didn't like to admit that he hadn't the faintest idea what Omsk was on about. "Well, I must get back to my study."

"Why have you no sledskis?" Omsk asked Bungo, Wellington, Orinoco and Tomsk. But they didn't know what he meant either. Omsk tried Tobermory who, as usual, was busy in his Workshop.

"Sled-what?" said Tobermory, scratching his head. "Never heard of it, young Omsk. What is it, a sort of sledge?"

"*Tck tck tck,*" said Omsk. "There is old wooden chair, yes?"

"Yes?" admitted Tobermory, looking at the chair Omsk was pointing at.

"Here is old pieces of bicycle metal frames, yes?"

"You could say that," agreed Tobermory.

"Put together is sledski!" said Omsk triumphantly.

"Put together is . . .*tck tck tck* . . . what a most unusual idea! I'll need everybody to lend me a paw. Call all the other young Wombles," said Tobermory, "and look quick sharp about it."

For the next half-an-hour the burrow was full of hammering and sawing noises and the sounds of Wombles arguing and talking. It grew so loud that Great Uncle Bulgaria went to see what could be going on. And when he did see his sharp old eyes became as round as his spectacles. For there in the middle of the Workshop floor was a chair on skis with long reins attached to the arms of the chair.

"It's your SLEDSKI, Great Uncle Bulgaria." Everybody said it at once.

"Dear me, fancy that, well, well," said Great Uncle Bulgaria.

"My very own sledski, *just* what I wanted. Who is going to take me out for a little ride then? You, Omsk?"

"Please," said Omsk.

So a few minutes later the very first ever sledski to be seen on Wimbledon Common was sliding smoothly over the snow with Great Uncle Bulgaria sitting in it holding the reins. And pulling him along very proudly indeed was Omsk on his wooden skis.

"Haven't enjoyed myself so much in years," said Great Uncle Bulgaria. "I always *did* like snow. Faster, Omsk, faster." And away went Great Uncle Bulgaria in a perfect flurry of snow, while all the Wimbledon Wombles cheered both him and their cousin Omsk of the Hyde Park burrow.

"Good sort of Womble, Omsk," said Tomsk. "Let's give him and Great Uncle Bulgaria three cheers."

And they did.

A Womble Riddle-me-ree

My first is in marmalade and also in jam,
My second's in pear and also in flan,
My third is in dandelion, double you might say,
My fourth is in hawthorn and also in hay.
My fifth is in milk but not in tea,
My sixth is in chocolate, loved by Orinoco and me.
My seventh is in caramel and also in cake,
My eighth is in honey which busy bees make.
My ninth is in orange but not in peel,
My tenth is in plum and also in meal.
My eleventh is in wheat and also in harvest,
My twelfth is in treacle toffee, which Bungo likes best.
It's made up of food, is this riddle-me-ree,
To spell a cook's name, as clever as can be,
She cooks for the Wombles who live underground,
But her name sounds as if in France she is found.
Who is she?

Check your answers on page 76

Make a SOCK PUPPET

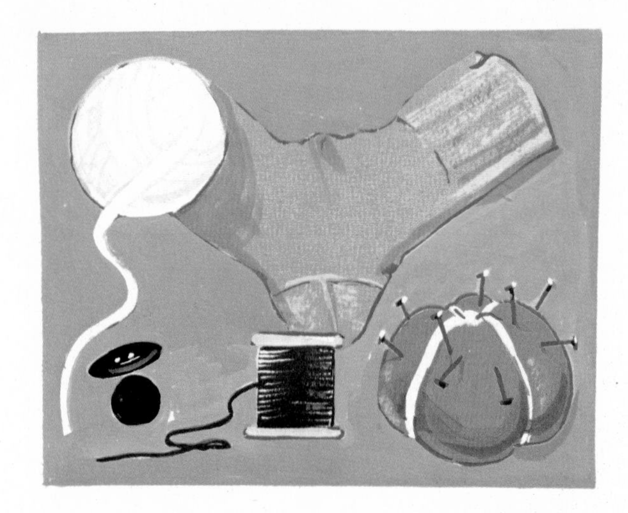

Here is a very simple Womble puppet for you to make. All you need is an old, clean sock, a black bead or button, a felt pen, and some white wool.

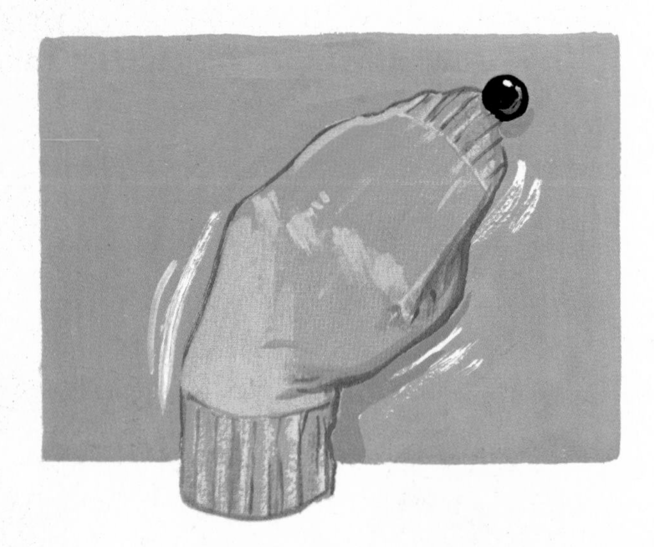

Pull the sock over your hand, and mark with a pin where the end of your longest finger comes. Take the sock off, and sew the bead or button to this spot to make the puppet's nose.

The simplest way of making the eyes is to draw them on with a black felt pen, but they will look very effective if you cut the shape out in white felt, with a black eyeball, and either stick or sew it onto the sock. If you attach the eyes over your knuckles, with a bit of practice you should be able to change the Wombles expression by moving your fingers.

At this point you could also sew on some felt ears, but again they are not essential.

To make the Womble's fur, thread a bodkin with some of the white wool, and start looping it through the sock until the head and body are covered. Every so often, do a couple of extra stitches to stop all the loops from coming undone.

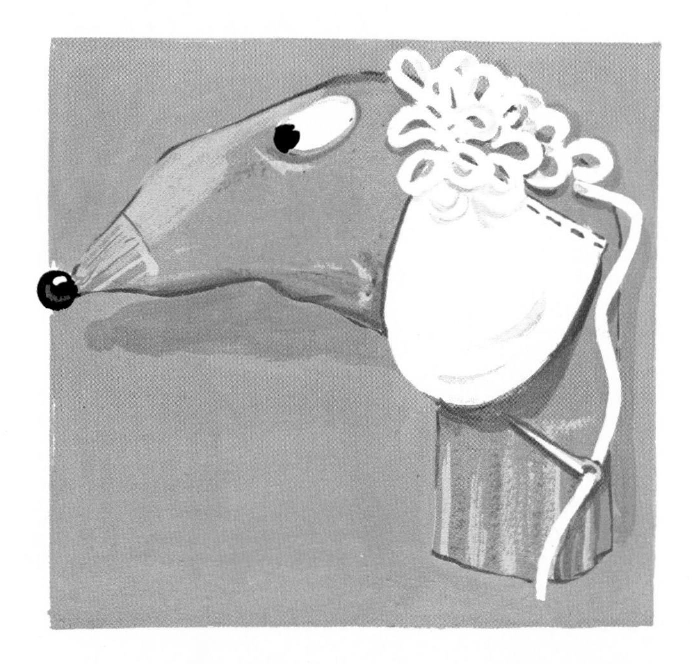

The mouth is formed by tucking the sock round your thumb, which you then move to make the puppet look as if it is talking.

This is only the basic Womble, however, so if you want to make all the different characters, try adding little touches like Great Uncle Bulgaria's tartan shawl, or Tobermory's apron, and then you and your friends can make up plays about them.

Name the Baskets

A number of the Wombles have gone hunting for litter, but they have left their own possessions in their baskets. Can you say to which Womble each basket belongs?

Check your answers on page 76

HAPPY NEW YEAR

It was three days after Christmas and all the Wimbledon Wombles were feeling rather bored and flat and even a bit cross.

Tomsk slouched around looking glum, Bungo told Orinoco that he was probably the laziest and fattest Womble in the world. So Orinoco refused to speak to Bungo and went off and quarrelled with Wellington. Wellington went off looking hurt, and then dropped one of Madame Cholet's best bowls and broke it. It's sad to relate, but Madame Cholet actually threw a saucepan across the kitchen, Wellington ducked and the saucepan caught Tobermory fair and square as he came through the door.

"Really," said Great Uncle Bulgaria, "with all this noise and clatter in the burrow a Womble can't hear himself THINK. Perhaps it will be a little quieter in the Womblegarten."

But it wasn't, for all the very small Wombles were being just as tiresome as the older ones and Miss Adelaide was sitting in one corner with home-made ear-muffs over

her ears while she did the *Daily Telegraph* crossword.

"*Ho-hum,*" said Great Uncle Bulgaria, "the answer to three down is . . ."

"I am perfectly capable of doing this puzzle without any help from you, Bulgaria," snapped Miss Adelaide, who in spite of the ear-muffs still had remarkably sharp hearing.

"I beg your pardon, Miss Adelaide," Great Uncle Bulgaria said stiffly, and he retuned to his study where he sat and thought very hard for some while.

"Post-Christmas blues are what we're all suffering from," he muttered. "Now, how do we get over them?"

He was staring at the wall as he spoke and slowly he noticed two quite separate things. A picture postcard which the MacWomble had sent them from Scotland with "Happy Hogmanay" written on it, and a brand new 1977 Calendar.

"Got it!" said Great Uncle Bulgaria, and reaching for his pen he began to write very fast indeed, with the result that the next morning the

Wombles found a notice pinned up in the burrow.

GRAND HOGMANAY PARTY.
ALL WELCOME. SPECIAL FOOD.
SPECIAL EVENTS. GRAND 'MY
NEW YEAR RESOLUTION IS . . .'
COMPETITION.

There then followed a list of names with times against them. The first was: Tobermory 9 a.m.

Everybody stopped arguing and being cross and a buzz of interest went round the burrow.

"What is all this, Bulgaria?" asked Tobermory as he reported at 9 a.m. sharp.

"It's my plan for making all of us greet the New Year in a happy spirit. I've looked up Hogmanay in my Womble Encyclopedia and this is what we're going to do."

Great Uncle Bulgaria talked for some time and at the finish Tobermory said, "All right. I'll do it. It seems a bit daft when I've got so much work on hand, but . . ."

"Ah," said Great Uncle Bulgaria, "stop grumbling, Tobermory. Remember the grand 'My New Year Resolution Is . . .' competition. Now off you go and find those bells, and kindly ask Madame Cholet to step into my study. She is my 9.30 appointment."

Madame Cholet talked in much the same way as Tobermory had done and so did Miss Adelaide, and indeed all the other Wombles, as they were given their orders.

"We don't giggle and play about," said Alderney and Shan-si together. "Do we?"

"Yes, but I'm not bossy, *am* I?" asked Bungo anxiously.

"You can be," replied Tomsk, "but I don't sulk, *do* I?"

"Sometimes," said Wellington, "and I'm sorry to ask you, but *do* I keep on apologising in a maddening sort of way?"

"Yes," said Orinoco, "you do. All the time. But anyway I'm not lazy. I just need forty winks to keep up my strength until mealtimes. I *do* need 'em, don't I?"

"No, no, no, you don't. And stand up straight when you're talking to me," snapped Miss Adelaide. "Imagine anybody accusing me of being too strict. Why it's nonsense, don't you agree, Madame Cholet?"

"*Tiens, alors,*" replied Madame Cholet, "it is not for me to say. As for me, I *never* lose my temper. At least hardly ever. . . . Excuse me, I have work to do. . . ."

Everybody, it seemed, had work to do. Tobermory was hammering away in his Workshop making a set of bells out of old cans and bits of tin. Miss Adelaide took all the Womble-garten out on the Common to look for pieces of coal – which were very hard to find – and silver coins. Alderney and Shan-si spent their time in the Workshop sewing together pieces of black material, and as for Orinoco, Bungo, Welling-ton and Tomsk, they had their paws more than full trying to follow the directions which Great Uncle Bul-garia had given them. Every now and again they would put their heads together and chant some strange-sounding poetry.

It was all very odd, but one thing was certain. All of them were much happier and nicer to each other than they had been.

On the 31st of December the burrow was a perfect hive of activity for, following Great Uncle Bulgaria's Hogmanay Plan, everything had to be cleaned from top to bottom. As this was very tiring work everybody then had a nice 80 winks until eleven p.m. Then they all got up, and with a great deal of whispering and laughing each Womble wrote something on a piece of paper and put it in a big box which had 'MY NEW YEAR RESOLUTION IS . . .' COMPETITION written on the side.

As midnight drew near a really delicious smell of cooking wafted through the burrow, for Madame Cholet was making a 'black stew' of bracken, bark and moss. Plates of grass and leaf shortbread and her own special steaming blackberry and acorn juice, with dollops of daisy cream to be added later.

"Everybody together now," ordered Great Uncle Bulgaria at two minutes to midnight. And everybody was there . . . except for Wellington, Tomsk, Orinoco and Bungo, who had mysteriously vanished. All the others held their breath and then, on the stroke of midnight . . . .

"Ding-dong, ding-dong. Dong-ding, dong-DINGGGGG."

It was the sound of Tobermory's

home-made bells ringing in the New Year and, as the sound died away, there was a tremendous knocking on the front door of the burrow. Shan-si and Alderney rushed to open it and everybody gasped, for there on the doorstep were four young Wombles wearing black hoods and long coats, and in each paw they held a piece of coal and a silver coin.

"The – er – dark – er – 'strangers' bearing New Year gifts," said Great Uncle Bulgaria. "Advance, friends."

The four 'strangers' shuffled in, took a deep breath and said together, "We are the 'first footers'. Here's tae ye and whae's like ye. May your lum always reek. Happy New Year."

"That means," said Great Uncle Bulgaria, "we are the first over this doorstep in 1977. Here's to *your* good health, and good health to all other Wombles and may you all be cosy, friendly and happy. It's a very rough translation of an old Scottish toast. Welcome home, Bungo, Wellington,

Orinoco and Tomsk, and Happy New Year to all of us. I give you a toast to all Wombles everywhere! Let the Hogmanay party begin!"

And what a party it was, because when they'd all had plenty to eat and drink, they danced Scottish Womble reels, including *The Dashing White Womble, We'll Take the MacWimbledon Road* and *Wombles of the Isles.*

"Well," said Great Uncle Bulgaria, as everybody was by now panting for breath. "The Grand New Year Resolution Competition. As you know, all of you have put one 1977 resolution into this box. All we have to do is to guess which resolution belongs to which Womble. Miss Adelaide, perhaps you would be good enough to draw the papers out of the box."

ANSWERS

WHICH BUSY WOMBLE
Alderney

WOMBLE WORDS
Across: 1. core 7. Wellington 8. kite
Down: 1. Cholet 2. tins 3. wall 4. money 5. litter 6. donkey

WHAT DO YOU KNOW ABOUT THE WOMBLES?
1. Hyde Park. 2. Cousin Botany. 3. WOM 1. 4. Tomsk. 5. Bungo. 6. Shansi. 7. Miss Adelaide. 8. Wellington. 9. Madame Cholet. 10. A Botany Burger.

PICTURE WOMBLES
1. Orinoco 2. Tomsk 3. Bungo.

WOMBLES IN RHYME
1. Orinoco 2. Tobermory 3. Tomsk 4. Cousin Yellowstone.

WELLINGTON WANTS TO KNOW

The Snow Womble
1. Great Uncle Bulgaria 2. Tomsk 3. Orinoco 4. Tobermory

Picture Names
1. Yellowstone 2. Wellington 3. Tomsk

Name the Tree
Hawthorn

WANDERING WOMBLES
Yellowstone: United States. Bungo: Wimbledon. MacWomble the Terrible: Scotland. Botany: Australia.

COUNT WITH THE WOMBLES
1. Four 2. Two 3. Two 4. Three 5. Five 6. Two

CHRISTMAS SILHOUETTES
1. Christmas cake 2. Crackers 3. Christmas tree 4. Christmas stocking 5. Christmas pudding 6. Bunch of grapes.

A BUSY LITTLE WOMBLE
Wellington

I SPY SOMETHING BEGINNING WITH 'W'...
Wallaby Walrus Whale Wolf
Weasel Womble

WOMBLE RIDDLE-ME-REE
Madame Cholet

NAME THE BASKET
A – Orinoco B – Tomsk C – Tobermory D – Great Uncle Bulgaria E – Yellowstone Womble

Miss Adelaide nodded and pulled out the first paper.

"I won't grumble all the time. Only part of it," she read out.

"TOBERMORY," everybody shouted.

"We won't giggle and play about. . . ."

"ALDERNEY and SHAN-SI!"

"Shan't sulk."

"TOMSK!"

"I'm not really bossy, but won't be."

"BUNGO."

"*Tiens, alors.* To be of a better temper."

"MADAME CHOLET."

"To work harder, eat less. Well, a little bit less . . . perhaps."

"ORINOCO!"

"Stop apologising. Sorry."

"WELLINGTON."

"To be somewhat more lenient, but only on special occasions."

"MISS ADELAIDE."

"Going to make less – less NOSE! I think that's intended to be NOISE. *Tck tck tck.*"

"THE WOMBLEGARTEN."

"Dear me," said Great Uncle Bulgaria as the laughter and the clapping died away. "I think you've ALL won. So who is going to get the prize? *Ho-hum.* What shall we do?"

There was a moment's silence and then a very small Womble at the back said, "But, Great Uncle Bulgaria, YOU haven't made a New Year resolution."

"I haven't indeed," agreed Great Uncle Bulgaria. "Because, to be honest, I couldn't think of one. Perhaps you'll all think of it for me sometime in 1977. But until that moment comes – let's get on with the party! And you know I think there are really enough prizes for everyone in the meantime. Happy 1977, Wombles!"

And there were enough prizes, it was a wonderful party and it was a very happy Hogmanay start to the New Year.

WOMBLING HOME

Any stranger wandering into the Wombles' burrow by mistake would have a very difficult task finding his way out again, especially if he wandered in too far. And even someone who'd gone into the burrow for a purpose – say to look for Uncle Bulgaria's study, or Tobermory's workshop – would have a lot of trouble. It's just like a maze ....

Here's a map of the Wombles' burrow under Wimbledon Common. See if you can find your way to Uncle Bulgaria's study by going along the right corridors and following any instructions, if you land on an instruction square.

HOW TO PLAY

Up to four players can play this game. You'll need a counter or a coloured button for each of them and a dice to throw. You have to throw a six to start.

The first person to knock on Uncle Bulgaria's study door is the winner.

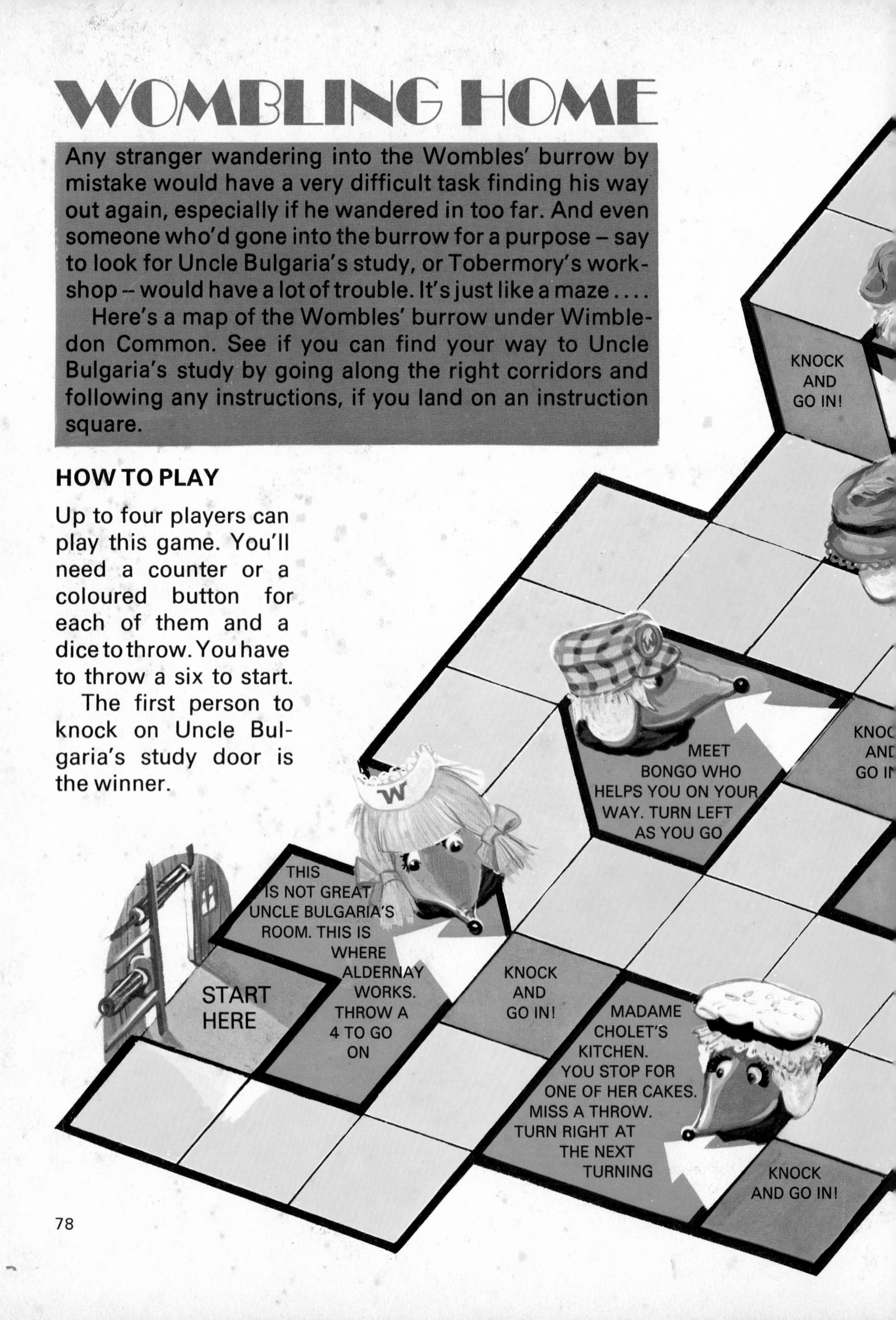